The Beginning

The Start of it all

My name is Simodore Jackson (pronounced syme-o-door). I've always hated my name ever since I was a child, most people have always called me Simon since my name is so hard to pronounce. I remember waking up and looking at my alarm clock at 12:24am, knowing that it was set to go off at 3:30am, which meant that it was time for me to go into my private room and"pray". I knew that what I was doing was wrong but I knew that in order to keep my current status of "Leadership", I had to. The problem was that I was not praying to the God that the bible speaks of, or to the God that all of my congregation was praying to. I was actually summoning demons, and I knew it. Did my conviction ever strengthen me to change? Well, I would say no at the time. This is the thing that I want you to see, rather than understand. My life, before realizing my call from God as a prophet was mediocre. I worked at a retail store in the shoe department and I hated every existence of my being, I always knew that I wanted more and that God had more for me but I never knew how to tap into it. I grew up with religious parents but they never really knew God. While my mother was a christian, my father was a practicing buddhist. So you can see how I never really took anything that they said seriously, pertaining to who God really was. There were times where I would get off of work and ask God who

He was and what I was supposed to do with my life, because I knew that selling shoes was not my passion. I wanted more. This is my story and now that I've lived it, I wish that I could go back and start over, you know, to please God with what He first gave me. Let me remind you that if God gives you a gift, a ministry or a blessing, it's up to you to do right with it. He gives you the option to choose between good and evil. Now back to my reality. This is how it all began. It was a Thursday evening, I was getting off of work and leaving for the day, when I saw a gentleman in the parking lot of the mall that I worked at, he had a flat tire and it looked like he didn't have a spare. He was standing outside of his car waiting for someone to come to bring him a tire. Now, my first thought was "that's his problem" but since I had been trying to get closer to God, I knew that helping him would mean that I was helping God and that helping another person would please God. So as I approached him with my work uniform on, I asked if he needed anything and he said that he was waiting for someone to assist him with a tire but that he didn't know how long that they'd be. So I then offered to call a friend of mine who also worked at the sears but in the tire department. I knew that my friend had worked on cars and also had helped me in the past with my car and that he had a small shop in his garage at his house which wasn't far away. Reluctantly, the man took up my offer and my friend who was actually off of work that day came with the tire that he needed. As my friend arrived about 25 minutes later, the guy thanked me with a 50 dollar bill. I rejected it, because I wanted to show God that I was serious about helping people. The man then told me that his name was Ron, but that most people called him Pastor Ronald. I immediately froze and said " wow I would have never guessed that you were a pastor". His next words shook me to my very soul and caused a shift in my spirit. He said "The Lord does not look at the things that man looks at, man looks at the outward appearance, but God looks at the heart". I was dumbfounded. So I told him that I felt like I wanted to know more about God and what my purpose in life was. He then said that It would be revealed to me if I came to his church that following Sunday. So we engaged in a deeper conversation and at the end of our meeting, I just knew that it was not by accident, so I asked him for his number and the address to his church. Again, you can call me Simon and this is my story. I hope that you will be encouraged by it and notice the signs so that you can know for yourself that we all have decisions to make and that God judges every decision. "God is not looking for the people who have their lives all figured out, He is not calling the equipped, but He is equipping the called". Sunday quickly approached. I drove to the church and prayed before I went inside, asking God to show me my purpose. As I quietly walked in, I sat at the very back of the church without anyone noticing me. As the pastor spoke that Sunday morning with such fire and conviction. I knew that this was my home and that my life had a meaning and that it was up to me to figure it out. As the Sunday service ended, I made my way up to the front to greet the pastor but there were many men and women of God in between him that I had to get through first. I saw the respect, the anointing, the power and the gratitude that this pastor had received and I wanted the same thing. As I am telling the men and women of God that I knew the pastor and that he was expecting me, the pastor recognized me and yelled "let him through". I felt pure joy because it made me feel important, as many others behind me were trying to speak with the pastor one on one. I wanted that same recognition. As I spoke with the pastor he told me that he knew that I would come and that God was calling me. We then spoke about my gifts and my purpose. I told him that after hearing him speak that I felt strongly about the prophetic office, he confirmed with three words, "I told you". I immediately felt charged up and ready to tap into this new revelation that I had. I began to buy as many prophetic books as I could find, I went to the prophetic training courses that they had at the church, I even spoke to every prophet possible to see how this thing operated. I felt myself learning a lot of knowledge but I still didn't feel that connection with God. I remember calling Pastor Ronald on the phone one day and asked him if he would baptize me. I figured even though I had accepted Jesus in my heart, this is what I needed to do. Pastor Ronald scheduled my baptism, which was 2 weeks later. After I got baptized, I felt so refreshed, maybe I can't really explain it but I literally felt free and when I came up out of that water, I felt such a welcoming feeling deep in my spirit and I knew that I was now a part of God's kingdom. As time passed, I got deeper and deeper within the church. I had started going to the minister in training classes at the church and I felt like my life was really going in the direction that I had always dreamed of. Pastor Ronald even told me that he saw my growth and how proud he was of me. Things were going really good for me. I met a beautiful woman at the church and she was really on fire for the Lord and it caused me to want to seek God even more. Her name was Olivia Stanford, she was very beautiful to the eye, but what caught my attention even more was her seriousness for God. I saw her singing in the choir at the church with such an angelic voice, I saw her praying and worshipping every Sunday and it made me want to get closer to God. I knew that she was my wife but I can admit that I was a bit intimidated because I knew that she had tapped in a lot deeper than me. I had never met a woman like Olivia before and I had to make sure that I did everything possible to get her to see my heart. After service one sunday, Pastor Ronald invited everyone that was active in the church to lunch at a nearby diner. Olivia was there, I was so excited to see how she really was outside of church! My God, she was so funny, outgoing and vibrant. She had such a sweet voice but it was also powerful. Every word she spoke at lunch, I pondered on. I told myself that I am going to make her my wife. I also learned that she actually talked about other things, outside of church. She knew about politics, accounting, and even relationships. I was super impressed and it made me want to pursue her even more. We spoke briefly at lunch but I made a commitment to find out more about her because I knew that she could help me get closer to God, but also be my helpmate in the future. Eight months had past, I had gotten to know Olivia more, but it was only at church. I was praying, fasting and seeking God concerning marriage. As another Sunday service came, I got the courage to ask her out on a date, but I knew that I had to use the term "court" because "dating" seemed like a word that people in the world used. As we wrapped up Sunday service, I asked her if she would like to go out to dinner with me in the near future. Her eyes lit up, as if she knew something that I didn't. She said yes and set the time and place. When that following Tuesday came, I picked her up at about 7pm and we went for it. At dinner, she told me that she had dreams about me but that she didn't feel comfortable telling me them yet because the Lord had not released her to do so. We talked, shared our goals, spoke about what we wanted in a spouse and we even prayed together. I knew that she was for me, but I was afraid of the dreams that she had about me. Were they bad dreams? Were they warnings? Was it about my past? I didn't know. The date ended and I took her home. It was short and sweet but I enjoyed every part of it. That following Sunday, we were back at church, I kept feeling someone eyeing me from behind but I was too focused on Pastor Ronald preaching on elevation and moving higher in God. After the Pastor preached, they called an altar call for prayer. I glanced back and saw Olivia piercing me with her eyes. I immediately looked forward and that was the first time that I heard God speak to me. I heard Him say "She knows who you are". I was shocked. And I could not believe that I had heard the voice of God speak to me so audibly. After the altar call, church ended and I approached Olivia and said " Are you ready to tell me your dreams about me yet". She replied with a look, it was a smile and a smirk at the same time. Then she told me that she had dreams about us walking down the aisle with angels singing. I was so happy that all I could do was play it off. I tried to be cool about it but when I got home I screamed, yelled, prayed, cried, everything that you could imagine when a person is overwhelmed. I thanked God because He showed me that what I felt was real and that Olivia was indeed my wife. Two more months had passed, we courted, spent time together and she even met my family and I later met hers. Things were great, we sat together at church and I felt like it was time for me to propose. I consulted with Pastor Ronald about it and he gave me his blessing but told me that I needed to pray more about it so that God could show me how to go about doing it. Two weeks later, I bought a ring and I fasted for 3 days with just water and fruits and I had a vision of Olivia and I celebrating. I was convinced that the time was now. That following Sunday, service was almost over, I told the church that I had an announcement to make. As I had the mic in my hands, I walked over to Olivia, bent on one knee, I asked her to be my wife! She happily accepted and the church went wild in applause, screams and hoorays. This is how our journey began. Everything else was a done deal. We started doing ministry together, teaching and ministering at the church. We were even leading bible study services on tuesday nights at the church together. We ended up having a beautiful wedding at the church with friends and family and moving in together. Life was not the same for me, I still worked in the shoe department at the sears in the mall, but I felt God calling me to go full time in ministry. Things started to move a little slower for me after we got married, pertaining to ministry. I felt like I needed more. I called Pastor Ronald a few days later and told him what was on my heart and that I wanted to quit my job and work at the church full time. Surprisingly, he told me that it was my time! He put me on staff full time as associate pastor. This was it! I could finally do what I loved and get paid for it! Life could not be better. I preached every other week, I handled a lot of his paperwork, I was being sent out to other churches in his absence, I greeted members, I ran prayer lines, I felt like I ran the church. I still even held tuesday night bible studies with my wife. Things were going well for me, that is, until we got a new member one year later. His name was Henry. He had just moved here a week before. He was very well dressed, confident, he knew the bible well, he spoke in 3 different languages, he seemed to really know how to demonstrate something that I had always longed for (signs, miracles and wonders).

When he came, he joined the church really fast, I thought that he was just eager like I once was but come to find out he was a prophet and already knew a lot about Jesus, ministry and even how to flow prophetically. I took to him quickly, just as fast as he had joined the church, was as fast as I developed a friendship with him. I looked up to him, I wanted to learn what he had learned and how to perform such miracles. It seemed like he actually came and took over the church because everyone was crazy about Prophet Henry! Whenever the altar call came about, everybody wanted Henry to pray for them because they knew that they would encounter an experience (signs and miracles). This impressed me because it made me think that he was closer to God than I was. I trusted him and allowed him to mentor me, I no longer even went to Pastor Ronald with my concerns, I went to Prophet Henry. He was now a minister of the church, but everyone called him Prophet. Something that I knew I was, but I never really prophesied or healed anyone. Over the next 3 months, he continued to preach every now and again but he always came up for the altar call each and every week to pray for people and they always fell out, to no avail. I wondered how I could ask him how he got this type of special power and anointing from God, but I felt ashamed because he knew that I was also a prophet. Henry invited me to come to fellowship with him and his brothers from his former church in his old city, they were still very close and in contact. I followed him in my car for about an hour and 45 minutes. When I met these men, they were also all in ministry and they were all dressed in expensive looking suits, fine jewelry and spoke very highly of themselves. But one thing that stood out, was that they never really talked about God, Jesus, ministry or church the entire time that we were there. As the evening went on, we ate really good food, we joked, we laughed, we even talked about cars. I was a little thrown off because I always knew that "fellowship" was about getting together to dwell on God. But I kept it going and I kind of enjoyed myself. After dinner, the men of God told me that there were things that I needed to know if I wanted to be successful in ministry. I was confused because I thought that I was doing pretty well at the church and in our ministry. They began to tell me that there were secrets to being powerful and that when the time was right, Prophet Henry would show me. After dinner, as we walked to our cars to depart, I asked Prophet Henry what the secrets were. He told me that I was not ready to know. I was a little puzzled as I thought that we were friends. He told me that there are certain requirements to becoming a demonstrator of signs and miracles. He spoke about sacrifices, secrets, and things that I must endure to do what I have seen him do in the church. This conversation intrigued me to the point where I wanted to know more.

The Shift

Three weeks had gone by and all I could do was think about how to

operate like Prophet Henry so that I could appear more powerful. It began to almost become an obsession. I started watching videos online, reading different books on miracles and healing and I still couldn't get it. I asked God why I haven't done the things that Prophet Henry did, but I got no answer. It felt like God left me, maybe I started seeking Henry more than God and that made God angry. Or perhaps, maybe I wanted power, more than I wanted God.

I would come home from church with my wife sad, she knew that she could not fix my problem so she never said anything, she just always prayed for me. I loved that about her. It seems like as soon as you are starting to do good in life is when your biggest temptations will show up. Prophet Henry invited me to his spiritual father's house for bible study, I was excited and said of course, Olivia and I would love to come. Prophet Henry quickly stopped me and said that I needed to come alone. This is where the shift took place. I was confused but thought that maybe it was just a bible study for a men's night or something of that nature. We drove for 3 hours together in Prophet Henry's Mercedes Benz C300. In the car, I asked him why he wasn't married and what he thought about marriage. He then told me that he is getting too much money to worry about a wife. I couldn't believe the man that spoke so highly and holy inside the church had just said this to me. But I overlooked it, as most of us do in life. We finally

arrived after driving for 3 hours straight.

Pulling up to a huge mansion, I say to him "This is your spiritual father's house?" It looked like the white house, it was gigantic and it had waterfalls and all types of lights outside of it. I had never seen anything like it before. As we get out of the car, Security is at the front door and I'm like WOW! Prophet Henry told me to act calm and not impressed. He was teaching me things all along and I had no idea. As we get past the front doors security we walk into this house and it has marble floors, high crystal chandeliers, and fur rugs throughout the house.

Prophet Henry's spiritual dad comes down the stairs and welcomes us and introduces himself to me as "Apostle Johnny Letherly". There was something off about him but I could not put my finger on it. We went to the study of his huge mansion and talked about ministry and going to the next level. Apostle Johnny asked me what my goals were and I told him to start my own church eventually. He laughed and told me that I could have that right now if I wanted it but quickly brushed me off as I was about to ask him how. We stayed for about an hour

and thirty minutes before Prophet Henry asked me if I still wanted the

power that he had. I could not believe my ears! I was like absolutely,

but what does that have to do with us being here. He explained that

Apostle Johnny is the one who helped him get his power. I said how

can a man give you power? I thought that God gave you everything

that you've shown me? He began to tell me that there are things that I

must do in order to become wealthy, respected and established in

ministry. As I am listening, my stomach starts doing flips because I

don't know what's going on, I thought we came here for men's bible

study. Apostle Johnny walks back in and looks at Prophet Henry and says

"Is he ready"? And the Prophet shakes his head saying yes, he is

ready. I'm thinking to myself (ready for what). So as we travel through

the mansion to make our way to the Apostle's basement. There is such a

cold presence lingering around. It felt like a silent screaming in the

air.

As it all began, the moment that would change my entire life forever.

Prophet and Apostle started praying, more like chanting, if you ask

me, but in a language that I was not familiar with. I stood there looking clueless and just confused. I felt like I needed to get out of there but I was also curious about what was about to happen next.

Apostle Johnny told me to write my name down on a piece of paper and give it to him, so I did, then he took the paper and stepped on it. He placed it in a big bowl, poured some type of oil on it, lit it with a match and then quickly stirred it with a huge cooking spoon and they both started singing or chanting rather, again together. Then he told me to spit into the bowl and say one thing that I wanted quickly, I knew that this was getting bad, I felt so convicted and scared but I wanted to see if it was actually real. I said that I wanted signs and miracles and for people to react when I touched them whenever I prayed. They then prepare a bath for me inside of the basement. It was like the entire basement was set up mainly for these practices. I am not sure what was in the tub, as I did not ask any questions because Prophet henry had earlier told me to not act impressed so I figured I couldn't ask any questions either. When I sat in the tub, it was almost like a baptism but the water was extremely cold and the water made me feel tingly inside. They then told me that I needed to stay under the water for two minutes while holding my breath. I thought that they were trying to kill me because it was almost

impossible for me to do such a thing, I tried but then the first time I

came up after 45 seconds. They told me to try once more and if not then it was an indicator that I was not ready. So I went back down into

the cold water and held my breath for two minutes and when I came

back up I felt like I was literally going to die.

I wanted to repent so bad but I knew that I had displeased God

already and that He would not hear my prayer. As I am gasping for air

and sitting in the water, they give me a soap to wash up with. Apostle

Johnny kept referring to it as "hesitation soap". They told me that this

is a special kind of soap that is used to cleanse people of doubt, fear,

or hesitation. And that after I used it people would not doubt anything

that I had to say whenever I prayed for them. I washed up with the

hesitation soap as I was told and then after I was done they gave me

towels to dry with.

As I stood there shivering, Apostle Henry gave to me what looked like

a rock, but he told me that with this charm I needed to rub it on my

eyes before I prayed for someone so I could see into their lives, and

they also would not doubt anything I had to say because of me using the hesitation soap. After I took the charm, He told me to rub it on my eyes now, to introduce the spirit to myself. After I did that, he told me to repeat after him and once I did that, I was free to go. The bad thing is that what he told me to say was very demonic and scary. I knew that I was making a covenant with Satan himself and that I could never come back from this. I began to get dressed and met Apostle Johnny and Prophet Henry back upstairs. Once we were all upstairs they asked me how I felt, and I said I actually feel refreshed. It was quite weird because how could something so demonic make me feel so free. Deep down in my heart, I knew that I was going to hell but I was already in it and no longer wanted anything to do with my old life (if this actually worked).

Apostle Johnny went on to tell me that there was a place that I had to go to in a different state if I wanted more power and that there were other material things that I could also possess, but he said that it would cost me thousands of dollars to obtain. My first reaction was that I needed to see if this was actually real before I spent any money and traveled to another state.

Prophet Henry drove me 3 hours back home and not a word was said the entire drive back. It was an unspoken language that felt like now we didn't have to fake or force a conversation or even be nice

because we had known each other's secret now. As we got to my

house, he said to let him know when I was ready to make that trip out

of state, but he also told me that I could not tell my wife Olivia about

any of this, I immediately remembered! OLIVIA! Oh my God, my poor

wife is going to kill me if she finds out. So I agreed that I would not tell

her anything about him or myself, or even Apostle Johnny.

When I walked into the house, Olivia was sleeping. I took a hot

shower and went to sleep. As I slept, I began to have a dream of a

woman, she had long purple hair, sharp teeth and three nipples. This

the woman was unattractive and attractive at the same time. She was

physically undesirable, but something about her made me look past

it. There was something about her that made me desire her. The

strange thing about her was that I felt like I had meant her before. As

she stood in front of me in the dream, she took my hand and led me

into a blue ocean water. There is where I remembered her, in the

water. She began to tell me that as I was underwater for two minutes

at Apostle Johnny's house is where she was sent and assigned to me.

We were now in covenant and she would come to visit me in my dreams once a week and give me instructions.

As I am still in the dream, she tells me that she is from the marine

kingdom and that there is much work for me to do, in honor of the marine kingdom. After we finished speaking, she splashed water in

my eyes but this water was salty and it burned my eyes very badly.

As I woke up from the dream, I was terrified and my eyes still burned.

I was shocked because I was starting to see the evidence that

witchcraft was absolutely real, but I still had questions of why God

never came through for me in those types of ways. I had my reasons,

but I never looked back. As the dream shook me up, I still started my

day as normal. I went to the church while Olivia was at work and

handled some of Pastor Ronald's paperwork that needed to be filed. I

ran a few errands for him and I recorded a video for our weekly

commercial where we make announcements and speak encouraging

words to the congregation. I didn't feel much different, just a little like

a hypocrite and a liar. But nobody knew my secret except for Prophet

Henry and Apostle Johnny.

As I got back home a few hours later, My wife Olivia was home and

she kissed me and told me that she had a crazy dream last night! I just knew that I was caught and that I was about to lose everything

that I had worked hard for. But she told me that she had a dream that

she was walking in a park with the sun shining, birds chirping, and

flowers blooming, but that in another part of the dream she saw me

walking in the same park but it was raining, thundering and

lightening. This was confirmation to me that God had forsaken me

and that I was going to get exposed. But I joked the dream off and told

my wife that it sounded like she was Bipolar. I know this was bad, it

was God actually warning her about what I had done because she was

really connected to God.

Sunday came and it was time for church. Prophet Henry didn't show

up. I was confused because I immediately thought that this was all a

set up and that my power wouldn't work. As Pastor Ronald preached, he tapped me to pray before the altar call but since Prophet Henry

wasn't there that I needed to do the altar call as well.

I told him that I had to use the restroom, that is where I rubbed the

charm that Apostle Johnny gave me on my eyes like I was told. We

usually had a system after every service, where I would Pray as a

corporate and Prophet Henry would pray for people one on one at the

altar call. But now this was my time to shine and to see if what I did was worth it.

As I am praying, five people come up for the altar call to be prayed for. The first person was a woman, I laid my hands on her and she passed out, I was amazed and I felt like FINALLY I am the powerful man of God! I am the king! Finally! I began to see things about this woman and as I prophesied to her she would cry and nod her head yes at me. It was working, the rituals that I had did worked. I wondered if it was a one time thing so I waved for the next person to come, and again they screamed and fell out. The Third person started shaking and convulsing when I touched him, I had never seen anyone shake that way, but as I understood I was departing a marine spirit in him which made him squirm like a fish outside of water. The last two people I prophesied to, they agreed with every single word that I said. When I looked out to the crowd, My wife's jaw was dropped as she had never seen me in such a powerful action. After service, everyone started thanking me and telling me how much I blessed service today and how God is really using me. Although I yelled Jesus with my mouth, my heart was no longer with him. It was with this new found power. It was almost like a drug and I wanted more.

When my wife Olivia and I got home she told me that there was

something different about me but that she was happy to see me dive

deeper into ministry. She had no idea I was using witchcraft to dive deeper though. I started talking Pastor Ronald into having

conferences at the church. We would have a miracle conference once

a month and I would be the host, by this time they would call me

Prophet Simon. My name started earning some respect. People

started recognizing me as the Prophet who could prophesy your

whole life. I was becoming known in the church and at our events in a

much respected way. Prophet Henry hadn't been back to the church

in months and I really didn't care because I had gotten what I needed

and I didn't want to share that with anyone, not even God.

My marriage began to be more of a burden because I wasn't spending

anytime with my wife anymore and all she did was complain about it. I

wanted more recognition. So I started going into our guest bedroom

at 3:30am every morning. My wife thought that I was praying but I was

speaking the chant that I learned from Apostle Johnny, I was rubbing

my charm on my eyes and rubbing my hesitation soap on my skin. I

wanted more power. I wanted to be bigger than the President. I

wanted to be bigger than God! I would summon the marine spirit to come to me when I went back to sleep. I did this every night at

3:30am.

The marine spirit only showed up once a week but I still called every

night because I wanted more power without having to call Prophet

Henry in order to get in touch with Apostle Johnny. I wasn't really

trying to go out of state for this power. I thought that this mermaid in

my dreams could help me to obtain it.

Each and every sunday, I would pray, prophesy, and lay hands with

the same effects as before, people rolling around, screaming and

yelling, crying, some were laughing uncontrollably, convulsing and

even vomiting. I felt like I had really tapped into something that not

even Pastor Ronald could explain. Although he allowed me to lead here and there, I
started thirsting for my own church. I wanted to do things my way, with my own name,
and my own members.

Greed

I decided to reach out to Prophet Henry to see where he had been, but

what I really wanted to know is if he could get me back connected to

Apostle Johnny because I wanted my own church and ministry and I

knew that he was wealthy and had the "spiritual connections" to help

me. Prophet Henry surprisingly told me that he had a trip planned to

go to Vegas next month and that I didn't need to consult with Apostle

Johnny because the man I was looking for was in Vegas and they called him the "General overseer". He was the one that gave out powers to us. It was said that this man in Vegas was on a master high level, he was a

millionaire, he had multiple ministries, multiple cars, a wife and

houses for days. When I learned of this man's name I was completely shocked because I had seen this guy on t.v ever since I was a kid.

Everyone believed that he was gifted and sent by God but now I am just learning that he indeed was part of the marine kingdom as well.

Prophet Henry described it to be as a family. He told me that we were all family now ever since my initiation and he told me that he was

sent to the church to find me because I was special to God. I began to

tear up because I started to feel convicted again, but Prophet Henry

told me to snap out of it and that there was no looking back. He then began to tell me that it was my anointing that drew his marine spirit there. He said that he was on assignment to see if I would take the bait and I did. Now, here is what I will tell you like I have in the

beginning.

We all have a choice to make, to serve good or evil, to do right or to do wrong. As I am learning more and more about how

these spirits operate, Prophet Henry tells me that I will be on

assignment soon to go recruit others into the marine kingdom as well.

But right now, I must focus on getting my powers elevated so that I

can have more rank in the kingdom world. But respect in the church world.

Prophet Henry told me that I needed three thousand dollars to consult with this General overseer in Vegas and that I could come with him when he goes to get more power next month. I began to think of ways that I could lie to my wife Olivia about needing the money. I decided that I was going to just take it out of our account and say that I needed to

fix the car. She doesn't know about cars anyway.

I quickly get the money together and into our savings account so it wouldn't be touched. I ended up also telling her that I was going with

Prophet Henry to a men's conference in Vegas next month and she actually believed me. I called Prophet Henry on the phone and told

him that everything was set in place and that I couldn't wait.

This is it

Finally, the time has come and I am about to meet the "General". The thing about it is, when I met him, he seemed very different from when I had seen him on t.v since I was a kid. He seemed more feminine. At least, that's how I felt. When I learned that me gaining more power consisted of being with another man is when I realized that God still loved me enough for me to turn back. I Just could not do it, I realized that I had gone too far. God began to immediately convict me to the point where I regretted everything. I just wanted to come clean with my wife, repent and start over.

As prophet Henry got done with his session, I caught a cab to a hotel and booked a flight back home as I pondered on how I even got this far in life. As I am in my hotel room, I drop to my knees and I begin to worship God. I repented like never before. I felt ashamed because I had fallen so short from the grace of God. But in that moment, I heard the Lord speak to me, He said that I am still His. I could not believe that He had forgiven me, but it showed me that He knew how serious I was about repenting. When I arrived home, I told my wife Olivia everything and we both cried non stop while holding each other. She was sad but she believed in me so we prayed together. I felt like I was free again, when all I had to do was turn from my wicked ways, seek God, pray and repent. I took two months off from church before I ended up going back to Pastor Ronalds church. The Lord told me that I was not to be in leadership for the next 3 years for my disobedience. Things at home got better and I ended up giving Olivia most of the money back that I was going to pay the "General". I am blessed today to say that I will never look back and that God has truly helped me to realize that life is indeed short and

a gift and we must live right and live in holiness.

THE END